To: Sally

From: Santa

W9-BRF-966

For Pandora,
Diggy, and Isolde

Copyright © 2008 by Helen Cooper

First published in Great Britain by Doubleday, an imprint
of Random House Children's Books, 2008

Printed and bound in Singapore

First American edition, 2009

1 3 5 7 9 10 8 6 4 2

www.fsgkidsbooks.com

Library of Congress Cataloging-in-Publication Data

Cooper, Helen (Helen F.)

Dog biscuit / Helen Cooper.— 1st American ed.

p. cm.

Summary: A little girl eats a dog biscuit by mistake and
worries about the consequences. Includes recipe for
"human-being treats."

ISBN-13: 978-0-374-31812-3

ISBN-10: 0-374-31812-3

[1. Dogs—Fiction. 2. Humorous stories.] I. Title.

PZ7.C7855 Do 2009

[E]—dc22

2008024124

DOG BISCUIT

Helen Cooper

FARRAR STRAUS GIROUX
NEW YORK

Hungry Bridget stole a biscuit,
found the biscuits in the shed.
They were made for dogs to eat.

But Bridget . . . ate the Dog Biscuit.

IT TASTED SALTY AND SWEET AT THE SAME TIME!

IT TASTED GOOD.

Foolish child!

Mrs. Blair found Bridget there
with telltale crumbs around her mouth.
"Oh my," she said, and shook her head,
"you'll go bowwow and turn into a dog."
"Don't tell my mom," begged Bridget.
She wished she hadn't eaten that biscuit.

"I won't say a word," said Mrs. Blair, and winked.

Mrs. Blair's dog winked, too.

And Bridget thought she heard it say,

"I used to be a child like you before the happy day I ate a Dog Biscuit."

Bridget's mom was rather late.
While they waited, Bridget felt
an itch behind her ears.
Maybe they were growing!

Mom didn't notice a thing.
Bridget wasn't telling.
Mrs. Blair waved goodbye,
the dog wagged its tail,
and Bridget wagged her
new tail in reply.

On the way home

they stopped at the Butcher's shop.

Bridget sniffed the air, and tried a few little "woofs."

The Butcher smiled at Bridget's mom.
"Good little pup you've got there," he said.
That proved it, didn't it?
Bridget wished she hadn't eaten that biscuit.

Mom still didn't notice a thing.
Bridget wasn't telling.
But at suppertime she gobbled her sausage,
and gnawed her chop,

and spilled her milk,

and her brother joined in,

until Dad yelled,

"It's like EATING with a PACK of DOGS!"

At bath time Bridget was a wild dog.

At bedtime even wilder.

At story time she was so full of mischief Dad gave up.

Yet Mom still didn't notice a thing.
Bridget wasn't telling.
Though she wished
as she curled at the foot of her bed
. . . that she hadn't eaten that biscuit.

Deep in the night, Bridget awoke
when the moon was soon to rise.
She heard the sound of someone outside.
She smelled their scent as a wild dog can.

Into the light bounded Mrs. Blair's dog, calling,
"Time for some fun."

And
Bridget
went.

She romped in the gloom
with Mrs. Blair's dog.

They tumbled in the shadows,
and the vegetable beds.

Then Mrs. Blair's dog leaped
over the hedge.
Bridget went, too . . .

And was swept
on
the
night
wind
into the park,
into the dark,
to run and bark
with the rest of the
wild dog pack.

They promised a wolfish
Midnight Feast
to Bridget
and Mrs. Blair's dog.
Then the wild hunt
sped up the hill . . .
past the bandstand,
    the swings,
        and the paddling pool.

The moment the moon climbed to the sky,
the bandstand became a great meat pie

and heavenly sausages
rained from the stars.

And when they all had eaten their fill
they drank from the moonlit milkshake pool.

and Bridget was happy indeed that she'd eaten that biscuit . . .

UNTiL . . .

She thought of her brother,
her mom, and her dad.
A dog for a daughter
might make them sad.
She gazed at the great
dog biscuit moon,
and

HOWLED

so

LOUDLY,

made

so much

DiN,

that the moon

the

moon

EXPLODED

and
the
sky

FELL

iN.

Gone were the hounds.
Gone was the moon.
Bridget found herself back in her room
with a mom who had noticed
that something was wrong.
So at last . . .
Bridget told Mom about eating that biscuit.

"Mrs. Blair was teasing," said Mom.

"She wasn't," sniffed Bridget. "Can't you see?"

"Not very well in the dark," smiled Mom,
"but you smell like my little girl to me.
Could we curl up like puppies,
just us two?
And tomorrow
we'll ask Mrs. Blair what to do."

Bridget felt girlish again the next day
but they visited Mrs. Blair anyway.

Mrs. Blair shook her head.
"Of course it was a joke," she said.
"I'm sorry if I worried you.
Let's go in and brew some tea
and find my tin of human-being treats."

That did the trick.

And Mrs. Blair's dog had one, too.

Human-Being Treats!

Ingredients

8 tablespoons unsalted butter, softened

1/2 cup brown sugar

1 egg

1/2 cup molasses

3 cups all-purpose flour

1 teaspoon baking soda

1 tablespoon ground ginger

1 teaspoon allspice

Icing and candy to decorate

Beat the butter and brown sugar in a bowl until the mixture is pale and creamy.

Now whisk together the egg and molasses. Add this goo
to the butter and sugar and mix well.

Sift together the flour, the baking soda, the ginger, and the allspice.
Add to the butter-sugar mixture.

Use your hands to blend everything together. Squeeze it and pound it until
you have a smooth, round lump of dough.

Next, let the dough rest. Cover it gently with plastic wrap and pop it in the
fridge for a thirty-minute sleep.

While you wait, grease your cookie sheets, preheat your oven to 350°,
flour your work space, then roll that dough. Roll until it's 1/4 inch thick.
Now it's ready for your human-being-shaped cookie cutters. (Avoid all
bone-shaped cookie cutters. You never know what might happen.)

Place your human beings on the cookie sheets, spaced about 1/2 inch apart,
and bake them in the oven for 8 to 10 minutes.

Remove them and allow them to cool. Then you can decorate,
with icing and candy.

YOU MIGHT NEED HELP

FROM A GROWN-UP.